THIS WALKER BOOK BELONGS TO:

_____

_____

_____

For Julia

First published in Great Britain 1986
by Julia MacRae Books
Published 1996 by Walker Books Ltd
87 Vauxhall Walk, London SE11 5HJ

This edition published 2008

14 16 18 20 19 17 15 13

This book has been set in Palatino

Printed in China

British Library Cataloguing in Publication Data:
a catalogue record for this book is available from the British Library

ISBN 978-1-4063-1328-4

www.walker.co.uk

Piggybook

Anthony Browne

WALKER BOOKS

AND SUBSIDIARIES

LONDON · BOSTON · SYDNEY · AUCKLAND

Mr Piggott lived with his two sons, Simon and Patrick, in a nice house with a nice garden, and a nice car in the nice garage. Inside the house was his wife.

"Hurry up with the breakfast, dear," he called every morning, before he went off to his very important job.

"Hurry up with the breakfast, Mum," Simon and Patrick
called before they went off to their very important school.

After they left the house, Mrs Piggott washed all the breakfast things …

made all the beds …

vacuumed all the carpets …

and then she went to work.

"Hurry up with the meal, Mum,"
   the boys called every evening when they
   came home from their very important school.

"Hurry up with the meal, old girl,"
   Mr Piggott called every evening when he
   came home from his very important job.

As soon as they had eaten,
Mrs Piggott washed the dishes ...

washed the clothes ...

did the ironing ...

and then she cooked some more.

One evening when the boys got home from school there was no-one to greet them.

"Where's Mum?" demanded Mr Piggott
when he got home from work.

She was nowhere to be found.
On the mantelpiece was an envelope.
Mr Piggott opened it.
Inside was a piece of paper.

"But what shall we do?" said Mr Piggott.
They had to make their own meal.
It took hours.
And it was horrible.

Next morning they had to make
their own breakfast.
It took hours.
And it was horrible.

The next day and the next night and the day after
that, Mrs Piggott was still not there. Mr Piggott,
Simon and Patrick tried to look after themselves.
They never washed the dishes. They never washed
their clothes. Soon the house was like a pigsty.

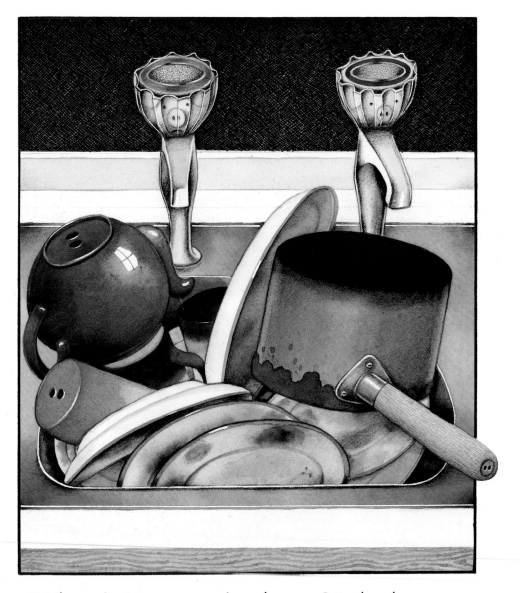

"When is Mum coming home?" the boys
  squealed after another horrible meal.
"How should I know?" Mr Piggott grunted.
  They all became more and more grumpy.

One night there was nothing in the house for them to cook. "We'll just have to root around and find some scraps," snorted Mr Piggott.

And just then Mrs Piggott walked in.

"P-L-E-A-S-E come back," they snuffled.

So Mrs Piggott stayed.
Mr Piggott washed the dishes.

Patrick and Simon made the beds.

Mr Piggott did the ironing.

And they all helped with the cooking.
They actually enjoyed it!

Mum was happy too …

She mended the car.